ABOUT AUTHOR

Abdul Aleem is a passionate writer of writers, a creator of remarkable works, and an innovative dreamer whose artistry spans poetry, prose, articles, and digital art. He has a passion for transforming complex ideas into simple forms and infuses the conventions of traditional storytelling with contemporary themes while introducing cultural insights into universal experiences. His creations retell stories of deep veneration for heritage and family values, with a profound sense of empathy and introspection.

In Abdul Aleem's works, there is not just artistic expression; his creations are heartfelt dialogues with his readers, inviting them to reflect, connect, and find inspiration in their journeys.

Written by: Abdul Aleem nsk

Edited by: Arham Faisal

Aleem creations !

The secrets

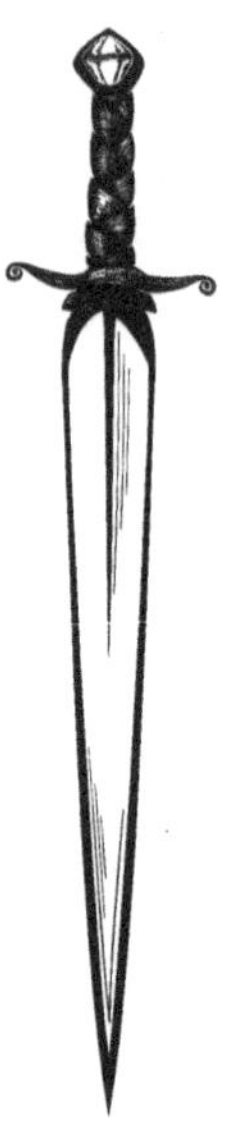

Abdul Aleem

Prologue

Joseph was a young boy living in a poverty-stricken yet calm African village. His parents, moral exemplars of their community, dreamed of a happy and prosperous life for their son. However, a difference emerged between Joseph's aspirations and his family's expectations. While his parents envisioned grandeur, Joseph found solace in simple pleasures: music, friendship, and the idea of living a low-profile life.

This clash of dreams and modest ambitions stirred a burning desire within Joseph. When his father's harsh words cut deep, they ignited a spark of rebellion. Driven by an urge to escape the monotony of familiar life, Joseph made a bold decision to seek a new path.

In his journey, he encountered a mysterious man of science—Steven Y. When Steven arrived in Joseph's life, Joseph was curious and eager to explore the depths of knowledge. However, beneath the allure of this newfound world lay a concealed taboo—a hidden skeleton that would shatter the façade of happiness.

It didn't take long for Joseph to immerse himself in the forbidden realms of knowledge. As he delved deeper, a dangerous power arose within him—an energy that could be wielded both to serve God and to destroy mankind. With each step, Joseph found himself sliding closer to the abyss of darkness, undergoing a gradual but inevitable corruption.

The path of redemption, however, was fraught with challenges. Joseph would have to summon immense courage, make sacrifices, and take risks that tested his

limits. Through this journey, he would learn the true meaning of responsibility, hear the call of accountability, and come to understand the heavy cost of power.

FOREWORD

They asked themselves, and everyone in their lives, what they truly wanted. Every story contains a secret, and every secret has the power to change lives. The Secrets is not just a story but also an exploration of people's feelings, choices, and the repercussions of their decisions.

Set in a small African village, this tale takes the reader into the life of Joseph—a young boy gifted with dreams who finds himself in mysterious and dangerous situations on his journey of self-discovery.

Joseph's story reflects humanity's attempts to overcome fundamental struggles: the choice to remain innocent or become rebellious, to seek knowledge or pursue power, and the consequences of every decision we make. It is a moving narrative that aims to touch your emotions and make you consider the unseen forces in life that influence our actions.

The Secrets encourages readers to examine their own lives from a fresh perspective. It challenges them to explore their duties in life and understand how courage can arise even in the face of adversity.

This story hooks you from the start, weaving a tale that blends humanity's struggles with the supernatural, drawing on our tendency to turn to the unknown when prayers and hopes seem to falter. It keeps readers thinking, feeling, and anticipating until the very last page of Joseph's journey.

Welcome to The Secrets.

Written by Abdul Aleem

In a small and peace full village of Africa there lived a boy named Joseph his parents were very rich And they were living a successful life and they wanted joseph to do the same but Joseph had a different perspective he loved to sleep listen to music and play with his friends all the time. One day his father shouted on him and said (You are the one who will degrade my image in locality .I was never like you ,my father was proud of me but you are the waste) now go and study said the father .The words said by josephs father penetrated joseph's heart

Joseph was broken and he did Not know what to do .He wanted freedom and he decided to leave the home . He left the home with some of his belongings. while walking towards another village he saw a man with a huge and attractive briefcase . while Joseph was looking at the bag the man observed him and asked Joseph to come and join . Joseph went with him and the man asked him "Boy you look so innocent .where do you live? The boy replied :I have no home (homeless). The man said would you like to live with me . The boy got surprised and said 'yes' . then they went towards the house . when they

reached there the man said "My name is Steven I am a scientist " when the boy listened this he was "stunned" and told him that I was not aware of your profession .Then the man said to him I was observing you and you were looking at my briefcase. the boy replied yes actually I was curious about the things in it. Then steven replied "you want to have look of it" the boy nodded. After that Steven opened the briefcase the boy was fascinated after seeing a pile of books that seemed old and rusty as if they were
carrying some magical powers. The boy already mesmerised by the view

of the books began to ask Steven that if he could read those books. The scientist refused his proposal but he offered him an opportunity for work. The boy excitedly nodded. The next day Joseph was woken up earlier by Steven and was surprised by the humble behaviour of Steven. "You can go outside for some amusement kid", said Steven. The boy was happy to have the opportunity to explore the town ,as he was eager to make some new friends. While moving round the busy streets of the market, he saw a beautiful girl looking so disappointed. At first he hesitated to ask something to her

.But after some time he gathered some courage and spoke to the girl in a gentle and nervous tone. "Excuse me miss you look so desperate what's the matter" .The girl looked at the boy and smiled gently . "Nothing I just lost some money with which I was supposed to buy some vegetables from the market"." I am so careless"." I can help you in this matter " replied the boy. After some time the boy found the lost money .It was stolen by a kid and was discussing about it with his partner. Joseph snatched the money from the kid and scared him. The kids ran away and Joseph returned back to the market lane where he had found the girl . After returning the money to the girl Joseph asked her name .Amber replied the girl . The girl went away with a smile in her face. The boy returned happily back to his home . Next day he went back to the market in search of some more new friends . Suddenly he was laid down to the ground by another boy with such great force that he could barely breathe . The boy with great efforts and struggle found a way out and looked down upon the boy who was angry and overweight". Why did you tried to hurt me, you fool ,you would have cut off my arm". "I don't care you fool took my money and gave it to the girl I will beat you brat" replied the fatty boy." This was her money . these kids stole it that's why I snatched it from them" replied Joseph." I ordered them to stole that bloody money. you dumb you are a newbie in this town that's why I spare you otherwise' I would have beaten you so bad that you would have cried all the night" said the fatty boy. "I don't fear you round potato" replied Joseph. The boy rushed towards Joseph with great velocity and Joseph was no match for him and was badly beaten by the fat boy . The fat boy went away with a big evil laugh. Then Joseph was helped by a girl from the behind. It was Amber. Amber sympathetically helped her to stand up. The boy struggled to stand but after a few efforts stood up. He felt ashamed and humiliated as he had been badly beaten up . This time he went back disappointed and spend a sleepless night . Whenever their was a work which required the boy to move out of the house he covered himself with a mask . He was tired by this type of living. That incident haunted him in his dreams almost everyday. One day Steven was missing early in the morning.

Joseph found it strange as Steven was always present in the house every morning. He found a letter undoubtedly written by Steven which stated that he was out of the town for some period of 2 weeks due to some urgent work. Joseph was alone in the house. He thought within himself that why shouldn't I read some books. As he was reading a book his eyes felt upon the briefcase which Steven carried during their first meeting. He was curious about it and opened it. There were 3 books which were the same as he had seen in his first meeting with Steven. One of the books caught attention of him it was a black and green covered old looked book. The most curious thing of the book was the statement written on it which bore the words "THE HOLDER OF THE BOOKS WOULD BECOME CURSED, ONLY THE TRUTHFUL AND PURE-HEARTED WOULD RECOVER". The boy was excited about it so, he began to read it. As he proceeded, he found out that the book was related to black magic. A line of the book caught his eyes. "THE POWER OF MAGIC WOULD INCREASE IF THE HOLDER WANTS VENGEANCE FROM ANY PERSON ,THE ENERGY

WOULD BECOME MORE DARKER AND POWERFUL". "Vengeance" said the boy thinking something in his mind. He began to read some methods of attaining the dark energy by the means of black magic. He read about a technique which when performed would yield dark energy. The boy had some bizarre thoughts regarding Steven but an idea stuck his mind. He thought of something and his eyes began to glow with green colour . An evil idea came to his mind. He thought of taking revenge from the fatty boy. But this practice of black magic required the name of the person which was to be harmed. The boy, next day came to know about the name of the fatty boy. His name was' Alex'. He thought of trying to weaken his opponent by the means of black magic and acquire some strength using the dark energy. So the last day he went out a distinct forest near the village at the time of dawn to perform the ritual of black magic. On his way to the forest his step fell upon a tiny lizard. He quickly jumped back in reflex and rolled down the way until he reached a place which was overloaded by thorny bushes. Finally he reached upon a village which was different from all those he had seen. He had heard about that tribal village from the people. The people of the village worshipped a different god . when joseph walked further he found a group of some different people who were praying the god to protect them from the demons . Joseph decided to move on ignoring all that he saw in the village .He found a cave and found it suitable for his black magic activity. He performed all the steps mentioned in the book and ignited the candles he made a pentagon on the sandy soil of the cave. He started doing the ritual with a mask on his face as described in the book. After the ritual was over, he waited for the result but nothing happened. "useless" he said with himself. Suddenly he felt an aura. It was like an aura of an evil entity. He had never felt something like that. He started to shake with fear. Soon after that a mysterious dark figure came out from the other side of the cave. It bore no face and was tall. It looked like the shadow of a tall man. Joseph was terrified after seeing this. He started to shake even more. He also began to sweat and started to move backwards in terror. The dark figure also vanished as it also moved backwards. Joseph stopped and tried to keep an eye on the figure as it started to disappear. The dark figure was gone and all the candles also ran out of the oil and their was only the light of full moon shining in the night sky. As he thought of retreating back to the village, he heard the sound of an exhale. In a fraction of a second he looked backwards and the dark figure was standing right behind him. It horrified him to the core. He was about to cry from fear. In a crackling tone the dark figure said "do not fear me kid as long as you obey me I wont cause any harm to you ". "who are you?" replied the boy.

shaking with extreme fear. I am the assassin of Dreadmere, "Zerath". You are the one who summoned me ,now tell me the purpose. The boy thought for some seconds and the boy replied " I want to take revenge from a boy named Alex. He wounded me and insulted me in front of everyone. "Alright" said Zareth. "you will have to bring me a hair strand of Alex then only I can punish him" said Zareth as he disappeared. Joseph packed all the things which he had brought and began to move away from the cave. undoubtedly returning back home. He was tired and wanted a quick rest so he decided to take a quick rest at the tribal village as he felt safe their. He slept under a tree thinking about everything that happened at the cave . "that fatty brat deserves a punishment. I haven't did anything wrong" declared the boy in loneliness. After some time he felt asleep. When he woke up the next morning, he was surprised to see that the tribals were leaving the village in despair. When Joseph asked a person about that, the person said in sad tone that the demons are now going to take up the village completely.

But their was a group of people who weren't in a hurry. They were seated in a large

room. When joseph walked towards the room to check what was happening. everyone noticed him coming towards the hall but no one paid any attention. But as soon as he stepped in the room. everyone looked at him in a strange way as if their was a strange aura coming from him. One of the tribal chief came rushing to Joseph and said "you don't know what you have done .

The devil has taken advantage of your feelings and he needs your help so that he can become omnipotent and cause massive destruction. The time is still in our hand, so don't make a deal with the devil or else you will lose yourself". The boy left the tribal village in confusion and his head was spinning with weird thought. Joseph reached the village after a journey of three hours. He remembered the task which Zareth has assigned him and he moved towards the market to look for him. While searching Alex, he found out that Alex was celebrating his 19th birthday.

So he decided to go to Alex the next day. Now he went back with an empty hand. The next day he went straight to Alex who was sitting at a broken bench outside a shop and was counting the green notes of currency. Joseph rushes towards Alex and attacks from the behind, pulls his hair and kicks him in the right. Alex was surprised but ready for a massive counter attack. He grabbed Joseph and began to beat him badly and kicked him so many times. He left Joseph, who was almost unconscious and carried his money and left the place.

But as soon as Alex lefts the place, Joseph smiles while lying on the ground as he had managed to bring a few hairs of Alex. "Fool! Victory is not in the fight but in the seeds you failed to see me sow. While you bask in your hollow triumph, my plan takes root—and when it blooms, it will bury you! Run now, hero, because the next time we meet... it won't be your sword that will break. It will be you" said Joseph before he laughs maniacally. He stands up, rushes to his home, brings the other materials required for the ritual and heads straight towards the cave.

When he reached the cave he found out that Zareth was already their waiting for him. He did as he was instructed and gave Zareth a single hair of Alex. Zareth took the hair in his hand and walked towards the centre of cave and closed his eyes. As he opens his eyes a star carved on the ground appeared with Zareth located in its centre. He performs the ritual in a silent way. After the completion of the ritual. Zareth said "meet me tomorrow". Joseph left the cave and rushed back home. He reached home at late night and slept with some regret in his mind. The next day Steven arrived back home.

He was glad to see that Joseph had maintained the house very well and everything was properly placed. He ate breakfast and decided to take a round of the market. He asked Joseph if would like to accompany him. Joseph nodded happily. Both of them left towards the market. While they reached the centre of the market, they heard a sudden sound of wailing coming from a house which was located behind a jewellery shop. They both rushed towards the house and found out that a woman was crying in the corner. Joseph's eyes felt on a person who was coughing heavily while being seated on a bed.

Steven was shocked as he watched the condition of that person. Joseph was shocked when he realised that the person lying on the bed was Alex. Steven said" the boy is in a bad condition , we must help him now and take him to the hospital". Joseph didn't react at all as if he was lost in some kind of feeling. The worst was about to come. Alex died in front of them and the two were traumatised. His condition was very worse. A white colour liquid was coming out of his mouth as if he was possessed by an evil spirit. Steven felt something strange.

A large crowd gathered around the dead to see what had happened there. Steven and Joseph left disturbed by what had just happened. steven also felt uneasy. Both of them went back home. Steven went to the study room where he had maintained all his researches and had also kept his secret books which he never shares with anyone. He opened his briefcase and was suspicious about one of the books being opened by somebody else. He was well known of the secrets and methods written in the book which can make the reader powerful if the reader chooses the evil way. He began to doubt Joseph for all this.

When they returned home,
Steven sat on the chair and said" Joseph what were you doing when I was at my work outside the village". Joseph hesitated for a moment and answered that he was just wandering at the local market. Days passed and Joseph wasn't feeling any good. Steven had also forgotten the event. But joseph had not slept these days as he had nightmares these days. But their was something in common in all these dreams. Someone forced him to do wrong things and when he refused to do so, he was harmed in a painful way.

The next day he felt something around him. He woke up and saw that steven was in a bad mood and he was doing something in hurry. Joseph asked him that why was he in a hurry. He replied that he had lost a close relative and now he has to go. He also handed the keys to Joseph and told him to take care of the house. Joseph woke up and said goodbye to Steven. Now Joseph was alone in the house. Suddenly his body started to tremble and he was shaking due to cold temperature. But this wasn't usual as it was summer season and it was hot outside.

Suddenly he felt a sound of footsteps. The voice of the footsteps kept increasing as if someone was approaching him. He was terrified and asked in a trembling voice" is anybody there?". No reply came, so he decided that he should investigate on his own. As he entered the main hall, he saw a terrifying figure at the other end holding a knife in his hand. Joseph was horrified and ran out of fear. But the dark figure chased him and at last caught him. It was Zareth but this time he had a spine-chilling approach. Zareth asked in a deep crackling tone " why did you disobey me?

Isn't your life dearer to you?". Joseph almost fainted out of fear but he gathered some strength and replied " Steven was here so I can't go outside without his permission"." Oh, you'll make it right, alright. But not because you want to, Joseph. You'll do it because I own you now. Do you hear me?" said Zareth. Joseph agreed and Zareth disappeared in the shadows. Joseph went away after hearing the commands of Zareth. He was ordered to bring some items required for black magic which included human nails, salt, blood of a dead person and some other requirements.

Joseph brought all these things but this time he felt sad. He had never felt so sad, but he was being forced this time. He brought all the items and moved towards the cave. he had at this time the feelings of regret and guilt. He was crying while in his journey towards the cave. When he reached the cave he saw Zareth was already their. He handed these things to Zareth and ran as fast he can. He thought of Alex during the time he ran. He reached home and locked the door. He sat there in front of the door and cried bitterly. He felt asleep at the same spot.

The next day he was woken by a knock on the door. He opened the door and found that it was Steven. Steven was shocked. He couldn't understand that how Joseph opened the door as soon as he knocked." Were you sleeping at the door? How did you opened the door so quickly?" asked Steven. Joseph replied in a hesitated voice that he ran to open the door. But his answer was a lie as it was clear by his body language. " Tell me the truth? What happened when I wasn't at home?" said Steven. " I don't know" said Joseph." You don't know?, is this an answer?" said Steven.

Joseph wept for a moment. Steven came close to him and asked in a gentle and humble voice" What happened? please tell me the truth". Joseph paused for a moment and told Steven about everything which had happened with Joseph. Steven was shocked to the core as he hadn't expect such a thing from Joseph. He told joseph that they must go to the hidden island right now or else Zareth would revive the dead beast which would cause massive destruction and corruption in the world. "Joseph, do you even realize what you've done?

You didn't just make a mistake—you revived a demon! Tell me! Do you have a plan to stop this before it's too late. I don't know was the only answer by Joseph. They both had their breakfast and they left their home. " Zareth will be going to the hidden island so that he can revive his master Azaroth and rule the world" said Steven. He continued" when you brought him the items he asked you for, he performed the ritual which made him powerful". Joseph's voice was trembling, eyes downcast "Steven, I didn't know what I was doing... I thought I was making the things right

But now, I've unleashed something that shouldn't exist. I see it every time I close my eyes—the chaos, the danger. This is my fault, and I don't know how to make it right."" Now let's fix this all" said steven. After reaching Steven stopped. He said that they must find a ship by which they can reach the island. " Where is the island? " said Joseph. Steven inserted his hand in his bag and opened a black glossy bottle. He picked up some of the black substance from the bottle and applied it in Joseph's eyes. Joseph was bearing the torment due to intense itching in his eyes.

But as soon as he opened the eyes he saw that everything around him was having different kinds of aura. But their was an aura which was different from all others. It was deep scarlet aura. Steven said" the aura you see is the passage sign of Zareth. He had just passed from here. " and if you want to know about the island, I know nothing about that, so chasing Zareth is our only option here" continued Steven. As they proceeded further, the aura started to fade and a veil of fog also started to gather around them. Their was complete silence everywhere. The fog was increasing as they proceeded.

The aura was almost gone. But soon as they were almost lost the sign of Zareth. the fog disappeared. With the elimination of fog came a strange island. It was neither too big nor too small. But it was clear that they were not alone in the island. They tied the boat to a coconut tree and went straight towards the heart of the island. As they walked for some time they reached near an old temple. When they walked towards the temple they found a dead person lying near the foot of the temple. The person was looking as if he was the guard of the temple. It was sure that he was murdered by none other than Zareth.

Be careful, this is the time when we are going to combat Zareth" said Steven. "Steven, I know I've done something unforgivable. I was blind to the consequences, ignorant of the darkness I unleashed when I brought Zareth back. This chaos, this suffering—it's all because of me. I was the one who provoked him, and I am the reason this nightmare began. But I won't let it end this way. I swear to you, no matter what it takes, I will put this right. I started this, and I'll be the one to finish it—even if it costs me everything, even if it costs me my own life" said Joseph. They both looked at each other and went up towards the door of the temple. As they reached the door of the temple they saw Zareth was already their, holding an Obsidian dagger in his hands." You are late" said Zareth." Look at the temple, how beautifully it is carved with the powerful black magic spells, I can smell the taste of your death even from now " added Zareth." You are the one who is going to die" replied Steven." You wish for my death, okay here is your present!" said Zareth as he stabbed himself. Joseph and Steven were confused as they looked in each other's eyes.

Zareth smashed his hand on the centre of the star which was carved on the temple floor. This star looking like star which Joseph saw when Zareth performed his first unholy ritual. The deep scarlet aura began to fill the temple and this aura condensed into a dark red liquid which initially filled the star and after that filled all the temple walls. The aura started to darken and eventually it became dark. This dark aura reflected a bright light which prevented the remaining two to see what was happening. But Steven managed to look from the corner of the eye towards the place where Zareth was standing.

But the dark liquid which filled the walls of the temple began to descend towards a particular direction. The two were now able to see. They were shocked to the core when they saw a mysterious and dark figure standing in the same place where Zareth was standing a few moments ago. And now in his place their was a dark and tall figure which horrified Joseph to the core. The figure had elongated and naturally thin limbs and his head was a hollow void. It was clear that the dark figure was no other than Azaroth. The two were more afraid.

Azaroth said two-three words, but these words were nothing other than a crackling whisper to the duo. Azaroth slowly moved forward and in a blink of an eye he was behind the duo and took a breath. The voice of the breath was clear due to absolute quietness in the temple. They reacted quickly and jumped away from him for their defence. But at the same time they were fearful of his powers. Steven had something in surprise. He had researched on the supernatural powers for years and he knew that how to control these powers by his will.

He also knew about the method by which they could lock this demon again in the temple. "We have to surround the temple with the black substance which I have stored in my bottle. This thing will prevent him from going outside the temple." Said Steven. "until I am alive he will not be able to get out of here. So your job is to divert his attention so that I can get enough time to surround the temple with the dark powder." Added joseph. Suddenly a dark spear attack Steven, but he dodges it. " we cant solve this problem permanently just by trapping him inside the temple since the powder wont remain outside for a long time" said Joseph as he started to worry. " I know of a method by which I can trap him inside the temple permanently. But I think that if we dust this powder in the centre if the circle above the star he would be trapped here forever. But it is a risky job." Said Steven. "Alright let's do this" said Joseph. The next which followed was a one sided fight in which Azaroth dominated and the duo was struggling. But the worst was yet to come. Azaroth had a dirty trick in his mind.

He started to manipulate Joseph and he reminded him of the mistakes he had commited. Joseph wasn't able to focus on the fight and was struggling to face the attacks of Azaroth. But when Azaroth forced his words in joseph's mind. Joseph let his guards down and Azaroth found it a perfect chance to strike. He picked up the Obsidian dagger and stabbed it in the body of Joseph. Joseph fell on the ground and was bleeding. Steven also stopped when he saw Joseph lying on the ground. But at the time Steven had reached the point where he can dust the powder and trap the devil. "Let's make a deal

I will spare this boy and you if you don't dust this powder. But if you do so , neither you nor this boy would survive. Steven agreed as he can't see Joseph dying in front of his eyes. The devil was laughing loudly. The duo was defeated. There seemed no possibility by which they can make things right. But when the devil was busy laughing his eyes felt on the place where he had kept the dagger after stabbing Joseph. The laugh slowly turned into a worry and when he slowly turned towards Joseph, he saw the Obsidian already pierced in his body. He was shocked. "you fool what have you done.

Don't you care for your life?" said Azaroth in anger. " I know that this knife is cursed, I read it in the book. And I am ready to sacrifice my life for the compensation of my mistakes." Said Joseph. " This is not the right time" said Steven as tears rolled down his cheeks. But Joseph insisted him to dust the powder, so Steven was forced to do so. The devil made a last attempt to get close to Steven to prevent him from releasing the black substance. But Joseph held him tight and they both were suffering from a great deal of pain.

But steven dusted the powder on the engraved star and the dark aura began to fade leaving the devil and Joseph going mad with pain. but Joseph didn't leave him and at last they both were turned to stone. Steven sat on the stone and was trying to understand what just happened. He stood their and cried for a moment. Steven stood up after sometime and left the place with a sense of great loss. He had lost a great friend an was now as lonely as he used to be.

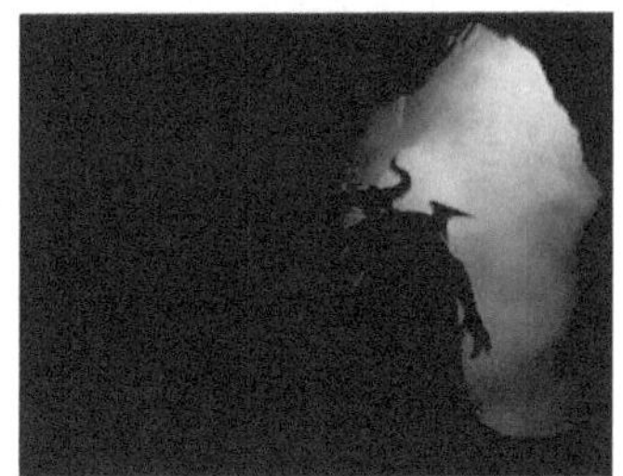

Joseph's parents, devastated by his disappearance, searched tirelessly for him. They put up posters in every nearby village, hoping for a clue. One day, Steven stumbled across one of these posters and immediately went to them, revealing the full story of Joseph's journey and the dark path he had taken. However, the truth was too shocking for Joseph's parents to believe. Convinced that Steven was lying or trying to tarnish their son's image, they handed him over to the

Joseph's parents, devastated by his disappearance, searched tirelessly for him. They put up posters in every nearby village, hoping for a clue. One day, Steven stumbled across one of these posters and immediately went to them, revealing the full story of Joseph's journey and the dark path he had taken. However, the truth was too shocking for Joseph's parents to believe. Convinced that Steven was lying or trying to tarnish their son's image, they handed him over to the authorities, accusing him of deceit. As Steven sat helpless in a prison cell, Joseph's parents were left alone in their despair, haunted by questions and regret.

Their hope for a joyous reunion faded, replaced by the weight of uncertainty and sorrow. In their hearts, they clung to the faintest hope that their son might still return, but the shadows of doubt and guilt loomed large over their lives.

"Every choice we make carries a secret, and every secret has the power to shape our destiny." Abdul Aleem nsk

"Mistakes are not forgotten; they linger in the shadows, waiting to drag you into the darkness of their consequences." — Abdul Aleem nsk

Read

The Battle Within book by Abdul Aleem nsk

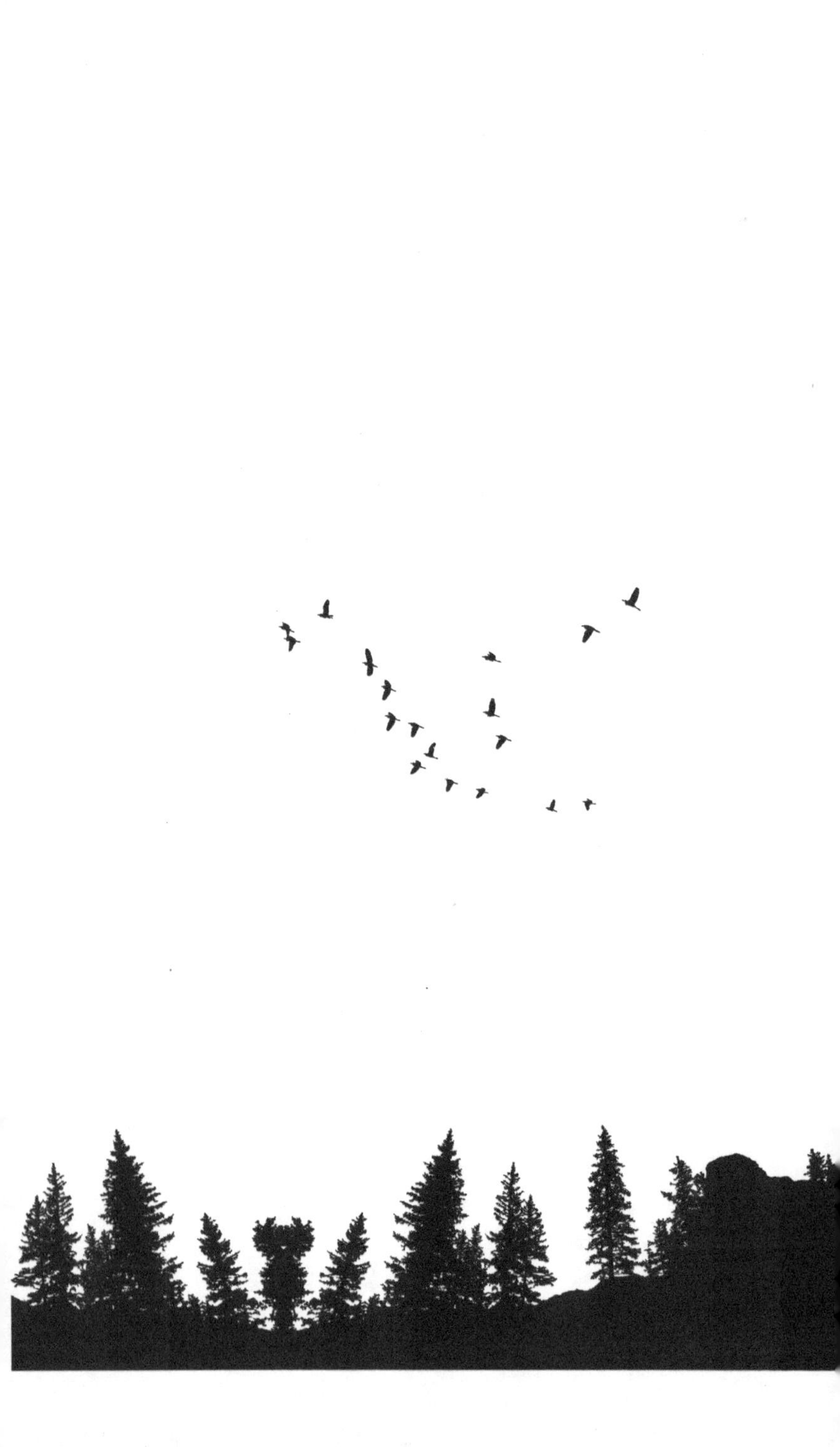

The end

www.ingramcontent.com/pod-product-compliance
Lightning Source LLC
LaVergne TN
LVHW040916150826
845672LV00007B/2079

9798897240036